It is not righteousness that you turn your faces toward the East or the

West;

but it is righteousness to believe in G-d, and the Last Day, and the angels,

and the Book, and the messengers;

to spend of your substance, out of love for Him, for your kin, for orphans,

for the needy, for the wayfarer, for those who ask, and for the freeing of

slaves;

to be steadfast in prayer and give zakah; to fulfill the contracts which you

have made; and to be firm and patient in pain and adversity and throughout

all periods of panic. Such are the people of truth, the G-d-fearing.

— Qur'an 2:177

Dedication

With G-d's name, the Merciful Benefactor, the Merciful Redeemer:
This book is dedicated to my parents,
Tariq and Zakiyyah El-Amin,
who instilled in me a love of reading and truth;

Linda Murray,
my high school history teacher;

my daughters,
Zakiyyah, Zahirrah, and Yaminah,
whose presence reminds me why this work matters;

and last but not least, my wife of twenty-five (and counting) years,
Dr. Aisha El-Amin—
my partner, my best friend, my peace.

I could not have done this without you.

A Note to the Reader

My introduction to history was not in a classroom. It was in my parents' house, where they kept a small library. Among their books was a three-volume set called Ebony Pictorial History of Black America. Those volumes showed Africa before the transatlantic slave trade, through enslavement, emancipation, and the civil rights movement.

It was there I first saw the scourged back of an enslaved man, the face of Emmett Till in his casket, Dr. King on the balcony of the Lorraine Motel, and Malcolm X after the Audubon Ballroom. I was eight or nine years old.

I was drawn to it, not like the spectacle of a fire but like seeing myself in a mirror. Drawn into my own story, its horror, and its beauty.

Today, there is a battle over which history will be told. The acceptable version is always the beautiful one, never the horrific. Sanitizing history leaves behind a palatable shell, making cruelty seem like character.

This book is a children's book for adults that exposes the absurdity and danger of such gentle lies. These depictions are rooted in real events, policies, and people. They show how polished words can hide brutal truth.

If we truly want healing, justice, and freedom, we must face the truth, unsanitized.

EDWARD HARWOOD

Legislator. Landholder.

Defender of Order.

From the Virginia Assembly notes, 1705, attributed to Harwood:

"Whereas the increase of free negroes and mulattoes breeds disorder, it is hereby decreed that no negro, mulatto, or Indian shall bear arms, hold office, or testify against a Christian. Servants and slaves alike shall know their station, preserving harmony within our dominion."

Edward Harwood was remembered as a devoted servant of the colony, a careful steward of property law, and a man committed to protecting Christian society.

SAMUEL DWYER

Interpreter. Loyal Officer.

Faithful servant of the Crown.

From the records of Fort Pitt. 1763. Samuel was praised for his "calm manner" and "steady hand in delicate dealings with the Indians." He spoke their tongue, conveyed their concerns, and delivered tokens of peace on behalf of his superiors.

One such gift. blankets drawn from the smallpox hospital, was offered under his care. Witnesses commended his diplomacy, noting how trust was preserved even as measures were taken to "secure the frontier."

Samuel Dwyer was remembered as a skilled interpreter, a loyal servant of His Majesty, and a man who knew how to keep peace.

JOHN WHITFIELD
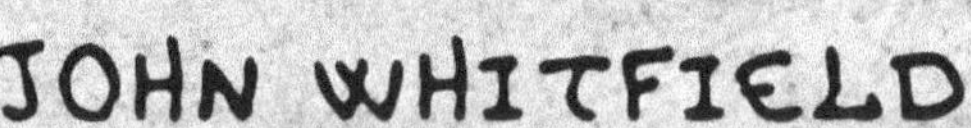

Husband. Father.
Entrepreneur. Champion of Freedom.

Born of humble means, John Whitfield rose to prominence through diligence and discipline. What began as a modest trade, returning runaways to their rightful places, became a thriving enterprise. With his earnings, Whitfield acquired vast acreage and a plantation of sixty enslaved souls, employing others in the noble pursuit of slave-catching.

In town, he was tireless in his defense of freedom from taxation and the right to self-govern. His words rang from courthouse steps: "Liberty is the inheritance of every man who labors faithfully and respects the law."

John Whitfield is remembered as a devoted family man, a successful entrepreneur, and a champion of freedom.

DR. JAMES M. SIMS

Pioneering Surgeon.
Mastermind of Modern Gynecology.

From the proceedings of the Southern Medical Association, 1852 — remarks attributed to Dr. Sims: "Through diligence and repeated trials, we have perfected a procedure to relieve the suffering of women afflicted with fistula. The advancement is significant, a triumph of perseverance and skill. It is true the work was carried out upon enslaved women, who endured the operations without anesthesia, yet from such sacrifices comes progress. Their trials ensure that wives and mothers of our nation may now live free from this malady. Science must advance, and it is our duty to lead."

Dr. James M. Sims was remembered as the father of modern gynecology, a man of courage and innovation whose work blessed generations of women.

THOMAS R. ELLSWORTH

Pioneer. Provider. Protector of Family.

From the journal of Thomas R. Ellsworth:

"Today, I returned from the frontier with coin enough to buy Mary a new kettle and cloth for the children. The reward for vigilance is just, and each scalp claimed proves our land safer for it. We build our homes with our own hands, and we guard them with courage. Tonight, Mary served stew by the fire, and the little ones laughed at my tales of the hunt. The Almighty provides for those who protect their own."

Thomas R. Ellsworth was remembered as a pioneer, a brave man who provided for his family, and a protector of his community.

SENATOR GEORGE KINCAID

Statesman. Protector Of People.
Defender of American Values.

From the Congressional Record, 1882 — the following is attributed to Senator George Kincaid:

"America cannot be flooded with cheap foreign labor. The railroad is complete, and the Chinese have served their purpose. We are responsible for maintaining the security and integrity of our nation. Wages must be preserved for American men, families must be protected, and our values upheld. Progress requires order."

Senator George Kincaid was remembered as a principled leader who fought for American labor and family values.

REVEREND DANIEL CUTTER

Pastor. Patriarch. Defender of Community.

Today, I preached on God's providence. I told my congregation how He blesses those who protect the purity of their land. The law that bars the Chinese from our shores is not cruelty, but order. It keeps our homes safe, our wages fair, and our children free from ungodly influence. After service, the women praised my words, and the men shook my hand. We are a people watched over by the Almighty.

Reverend Daniel Cutter was remembered as a shepherd to

his flock, a man of steadfast faith, and a protector of

American values.

Jim Wilkes

Family Man. Deacon. Strict Disciplinarian.

a loving husband and father. He's a deacon in his church: he and his family are there every Sunday. His wife, Sally bakes bread for the poor. Jim's a helpful neighbor—he helped old man Swilligan put up his fence after a section fell down, due to rot.

Jim works as an overseer on the Smith Cotton Plantation and prides himself on being a strict disciplinarian. Some of the unculutred, and un-Christian-like folk say that a few of the slave children bear a striking resemblance to Jim...but Jim is a good man.

Jane Keller

wife. Loving Mother. Socialite.

From the journal of Jane Keller:

"Dear God.
Today my eyes were brightened by the sight of little
Howie taking his rightful place. He made the boy John
gave him lie down to play "correction." Five well-placed
lashes with the whip he fashioned himself—each stroke
neat and true. across the shoulders and along the back's
arch.

One day. all of this will be his. Thank you for blessing me
with such a good boy."

Jane Keller was remembered as a loving mother. a
gracious hostess. and a woman of faith.

Daniel Cromwell, aka "Big Dan"

Strong man. Loving Son.

Daniel Cromwell, known to friends and neighbors as "Big Dan," left the lynching early—before the rush for souvenirs. Eight years ago, his mother suffered a stroke that left her unable to speak or walk. Ever the dutiful son, Big Dan never missed dinner with her. He would patiently feed her, humming her favorite hymn, the same one she once sang to him as a boy.

In the community, Big Dan is remembered as a gentle caregiver, a man who honored his mother with devotion. Some say the same hands that steadied her trembling spoon had, just hours before, helped hoist the rope. But to those who knew him best, Big Dan was a good man.

REVEREND PAUL H. DUNHAM

Minister. Community leader.
Man of God.

From his Sunday sermon, 1942:

"We must remember that every trial our nation faces is permitted by Providence. These measures, though difficult, are taken for the preservation of peace. Our Japanese neighbors are being relocated for their own safety and for ours. Let us trust that this temporary separation will strengthen their faith — and ours. True loyalty, after all, is shown through obedience."

Reverend Dunham was remembered as a compassionate shepherd, a steady voice during wartime, and a man devoted to faith and country.

ROBERT CALDWELL

Guardian of Public Health

From a U.S. Public Health Service report, 1942 — the following is attributed to Administrator Robert Caldwell: "The Tuskegee program continues to yield important findings on the natural course of syphilis in the Negro male. By monitoring subjects without interruption, we preserve the integrity of the study. Federal oversight ensures both order and benefit. One day, our nation's doctors will thank us for the foresight shown here."

Robert Caldwell was remembered as a loyal civil servant, a careful steward of federal programs, and a man of faith.

ABIGAIL HARPER

Pioneer Wife. Mother. Orchard Grower

From the journal of Abigail Harper:

Today, I walked through my orchard, thanking God for the land that sustains us. Little Sarah followed close behind, her hands full of apples. At night, I sit by the fire stitching a quilt from the new fabrics John traded in town. Sometimes, when John turns the soil, he still uncovers little arrow points. We keep them by the hearth or use them to strike kindling. Every piece, every stitch, every root in our soil tells me: we have built a home from nothing.

Abigail Harper was remembered as a loving mother and a pioneer wife who built a home on the frontier.

MARGARET WINSLOW

Teacher. Caretaker. Christian Matron.

From the recollections of Margaret Winslow:

Every morning I remind the girls that
God loves a clean heart and tidy hands.
I brush their hair smooth, trim it neat,
and store away the braids they arrive
with. I correct their speech when they slip
into their native tongues. We sing hymns
until they sound just like my own
daughters at home.

They resist sometimes. One little girl wept
for days when I took away the necklace
she wore from her mother. I told her
sternly that idols have no place in God's
school.

She will thank me one day.

Margaret Winslow was remembered as a tireless
teacher, a kind woman who gave her life to children.

~~the End~~

welcome to the beginning...

The Ugly Truth

Appendix

Edward Harwood (early Virginia)

In colonial Virginia, laws known as the Black Codes were drafted to define Africans and their descendants as property. These laws criminalized literacy, interracial friendship, and mobility. Oppression was written in ink long before it was enforced with chains.

Samuel Dwyer (mid-1700s)

British and colonial soldiers distributed smallpox-infected blankets to Native communities under the guise of peace offerings. It was biological warfare masked as diplomacy. Entire nations were decimated while officials called it strategy.

John Whitfield (early 1800s)

Slave catchers like Whitfield profited from returning escapees to bondage, sometimes capturing free Black people for reward. They called it "law and order." Freedom itself became contraband.

Dr. James M. Sims (1840s)

Hailed as the "father of modern gynecology," Sims perfected surgical procedures by experimenting on enslaved Black women without anesthesia. Their names—Anarcha, Lucy, and Betsey—survive as testimony to pain turned into progress. Medicine advanced through their suffering, not his mercy.

Thomas R. Ellsworth (late 1700s – early 1800s)

Frontiersmen were paid bounties for Native scalps, treating human life as a ledger entry. Official records called it "protection" and "defense." The frontier's growth was fertilized with genocide.

George Kincaid (1882)

Senators like Kincaid helped pass the Chinese Exclusion Act, the first federal law to ban immigration by nationality. They warned that Chinese laborers would "corrupt American purity." Racism became national policy.

Reverend Daniel Cutter (late 1800s)

Church leaders often echoed lawmakers, preaching that exclusion and segregation were divinely ordained. Their pulpits turned prejudice into piety. Scripture was used as scaffolding for hate.

Jim Wilkes (Antebellum South)

Overseers like Jim Wilkes were the enforcers of the slave economy. Their "discipline" often meant torture, rape, and public humiliation of enslaved people, including children. Many were praised for their loyalty and piety, even as they destroyed families.

Jane Keller (1847)

Women on plantations frequently participated in or sanctioned brutality against enslaved people, including children. Christian devotion and domestic gentility were used to disguise cruelty. Motherhood became a theater for power rather than compassion.

Daniel Cromwell (c. 1910s)

Lynchings were community spectacles in early-twentieth-century America. Participants mailed postcards, collected body parts, and sang hymns beneath hanging bodies. Their neighbors called them respectable citizens.

Reverend Paul H. Dunham (1942)

Many clergy publicly supported the internment of Japanese Americans, calling it obedience to divine order. Over 120,000 people were uprooted, their property seized, their faith tested. "Protection" was the language of persecution.

Robert Caldwell (1942 – 1972)

The Tuskegee Study of Untreated Syphilis denied hundreds of Black men medical treatment so researchers could watch them die. Government doctors recorded their suffering for forty years. Their trust was betrayed in the name of science.

The Ugly Truth

Abigail Harper (1830s)

 White settlers claimed Indigenous land under the illusion of providence. Every orchard and quilt on that land was rooted in displacement and death. Cherokee families were forced west in winter while "pioneers" built their homes from stolen ground.

Margaret Winslow (early 1900s)

Missionaries and educators like Margaret Winslow ran boarding schools that stripped Native children of language and identity. "Civilization" meant erasure. Many never returned home.

About the Author

Tariq I. El-Amin serves as Resident Imam of Masjid Al-Taqwa in Chicago. He hosts and produces The American Muslim Podcast and The Sanitizing History Podcast. and is the author of the Sanitizing History series.

He uses his platform to promote interfaith understanding. education. and honest dialogue that inspires reflection and coalition building.

Contact: SanitizingHistory@gmail.com